Agency
Confidential

Book 2

Cheat

Elka Dahl, Private Investigator

Liz Dodwell

Liz Dodwell

Agency Confidential Book 2: Cheat

Copyright © 2015 by Liz Dodwell

www.lizdodwell.com

Print ISBN-10: 1939860237

Print ISBN-13: 978-1-939860-23-1

Published by Mix Books, LLC

Table of Contents

One

A hundred and eighty feet underwater; the diver was thrashing helplessly around. Caught in the grip of nitrogen narcosis she had reached a state of panic. In the darkness of the tunnel known as The Arch, which ran from the Blue Hole to the Red Sea, she just couldn't get her mind to focus and her body felt heavy and slow. She wasn't aware of it, but her scuba tank had been filled with compressed air instead of the trimix she needed at that depth.

A sharp, insistent tapping on her shoulder abruptly distracted her frenzied mind. With a moment of clarity she realized someone was there, then the fear settled back in and she clutched frantically at her hoped-for rescuer. But her arms were pushed forcefully away and a bright light encompassed her. She froze. Was this it? Was this the light that signaled her life was coming to an end?

The light dimmed, then turned from her to show the face of the other diver, giving the universal sign of "OK," tip of thumb to tip of middle finger forming an "O."

The stranger gestured with a wide sweep of an arm and gripped her firmly at her elbow. She kicked with her fins but barely moved. Why did she feel so heavy?

Then the stranger reached for her waist and suddenly the weight was gone. Still groggy and addle-brained she struggled to focus 'til the other diver took firm hold of her. Together they swam along the dark tunnel 'til the waters turned a brilliant blue. She realized they were back in the Blue Hole and must be ascending. Her mind was clearing rapidly and relief flooded her senses. She looked to the person she was already thinking of as her guardian angel, but the diver kept behind her, guiding her upwards to safety and taking care to make decompression stops – pauses that allow time to release dangerous "microbubbles" that build up in a diver's body.

On the beach many hands were waiting to carry her to safety but she shoved them away, watching for her liberator to break surface. But the diver never appeared.

Two

It all began five days earlier. An urgent appointment with Elka's investigative company, Agency Confidential, had been requested by Isabell Kalb. She arrived promptly; a woman in sober, yet chic, business attire and with an angry air.

"I'll come straight to the point," she said, "I believe my friend has been murdered. The police have dismissed her death as accidental and refuse to pursue it further. I'd like you to find out what happened. I have a very successful law practice and am prepared to pay a generous fee."

Elka took in a slow breath, leaning back in her chair and crossing her long legs. She studied the woman for several moments. "Then you'd better tell me your story," she said.

The lawyer nodded, and began. "I first met Pamela in college. She was Pamela Vaughan then and we were sorority sisters. My family were well off, but not in the way that Pam's family were. For me, working was not an option, so as soon as I graduated I joined a law firm. Pam, by then, had met Galen Albritton. When he asked for Pam's hand her family were delighted. He was everything they thought she should have in a husband and they pushed for the marriage. I really don't think she would have married him otherwise.

"Anyway, they were married for seven years and had a daughter before Galen decided he'd had enough, and took off for Antigua with a lingerie salesgirl. Megyn, their daughter, was just three.

"Fast forward twenty years - to last year, in fact. Pam decided she needed some excitement in her life and went on a solo trip to Ireland. She came back with a husband…twenty-five years her junior!"

"Is the husband Irish?" Elka asked.

"No. American. Jase de Ville. Apparently he was also traveling alone. They were both staying at The Lake Hotel in Killarney and met sight-seeing at some castle. You know; stunning scenery, ancient Celtic myths, charming villages – all very romantic, especially for a lonely, sex-starved, middle-aged woman."

"And Pam was all those things?"

"Oh, yes. She was always insecure. And after Galen left she made up her mind that she must be unlovable and devoted her life to her daughter."

"Where was the daughter – Megyn, you said? – while Pam was away?"

"She was at the family home. Pam has – had – a lovely old 1800s farmhouse, modernized and with add-ons of course. Acres of land, adjacent to a lake."

"And she brought her new husband back there?"

"She even threw a party to introduce him to her friends. People she hadn't talked to in years showed up. They were all curious to see what would make a grown woman fall for someone hardly more than a boy.

"What's he like?"

"You know how some men just exude sexual energy? Well, he's one. He's not that tall, certainly not as tall as you," she eyed the six-foot Elka, "but he has a dark, dangerous presence that can be very attractive to some women. Can you understand that?"

More than you know, thought Elka, but to Isabell she merely nodded and the woman continued.

"I remember he was wearing a shirt with the sleeves rolled up high, and on his arm was a tattoo of a hideous creature, jaws wide, huge teeth dripping blood. He said it was a sea serpent.

"Anyway, I'm getting away from the story. Of course, everyone was sure the man had married Pam for her money, and she knew that's what they thought. So, once all the guests were there she announced she had a few words to say. She introduced Jase, then went on to say he'd signed a prenuptial that meant he would get nothing if she died other than a natural death, and anyone who thought he'd married her for anything but love was no longer her friend and could leave right away.

"Well, there was a shocked silence then the guests started to file out until there were only a few of us left. Honestly, I didn't know what to do. I didn't believe his motives were good but Pam was important to me, and I didn't want to let her down."

Isabell leaned forward, bringing her hand up and rubbing her temple. "I'm getting a headache. You wouldn't happen to have any aspirin, would you?"

Elka stood. "Aspirin or Tylenol?"

"Aspirin's fine, thanks."

"I'll be right back." Elka left the room but was back minutes later with several packages of pain killer and a bottle of water.

Isabell gave a weak smile of thanks as she downed a couple of pills. "Alright, any other questions so far?"

"Actually, yes," Elka responded. "Tell me about the daughter, Megyn, during this time."

"Oh, Megyn." Isabell shook her head. "She was furious with her mother; hated her step-father. They're the same age, you know? Megyn and Jase. They're both twenty-three, and I can't imagine it was easy for her. But she threw a terrible tantrum at the party – before her mother's announcement. Said her mother was a stupid bitch and she'd sold out for a 'hot beef injection.' It was awful; Pam was devastated and Megyn stormed out."

"She sounds like a troubled young woman."

"Pam always babied her and let her have her way. Suddenly someone else had a large share of her mother's attention. She was pissed."

"No doubt. But let's get to what happened to Pam and the reason why you're here."

"Alright." Isabell took another sip of her water and closed her eyes for a moment. "I told you there was a lake at the house. When it was warm enough, Pam liked to swim every day. It would take her about forty-five minutes to swim across and back. Three months ago, she began her swim and never came back. Her body was fished out a couple of days later. The autopsy report determined cause of death as drowning, and manner of death as accidental.

"There was speculation she cramped up and panicked. But I'm telling you, that would never have happened. In her teens Pam was a state swimming champion. She was still a strong swimmer and she certainly knew how to stay afloat if she cramped. She was seen by some neighbors who were in a row-boat, fishing. They called out a greeting, she stopped to exchange a few words with them and she was fine. They're the last people to have seen her."

"Where were Jase and Megyn?"

"Jase was at the house. The same people in the boat saw him on the deck and they waved at each other. Megyn had driven into town."

Elka steepled her fingers under her chin and gave Isabell a hard look.

"So you're telling me based on your knowledge of your friend, you don't believe she died accidentally, but you have absolutely no evidence that she was killed." She raised her eyebrows. "That may be a basis for suspicion, but hardly for investigation."

"I haven't come to the real shocker yet. After Pam's death, Jase continued to live in the house, with Megyn there. Then," Isabell paused for effect, "a week ago, Jase and Megyn got married."

At that, Isabell leaned back in the chair. Her face was pale and she rubbed again at her temple. Elka leaned towards her and squeezed her shoulder.

"I can see this is stressful for you. Try and relax and let me see if I understand what you want of me." She began to pace back and forth. "You need someone to look into the possibility of Jase's involvement with Pam's death. And I presume you fear for Megyn's safety so you're looking for some sort of protection."

"That's it exactly."

"If it can be proved Jase had nothing to do with his wife's death, would you agree Megyn is *not* in danger?"

"I, uh, I suppose. I hadn't thought of it."

"Why did you come to me?" Elka suddenly changed the subject. "You must have investigators of your own."

"That's true. But they don't have your reputation of fighting for women who have no-one else to turn to."

Three

Dahab, Egypt was unseasonably hot for mid-April. At six-thirty in the morning it was already seventy seven Fahrenheit as Elka Dahl stood on the balcony of her room at the Dahab Paradise. The first windsurfers were catching the breeze out in the bay, and looking down Elka saw a handful of people with scuba gear. The Red Sea offered access to incredible reefs and marine life, and the infamous Blue Hole – a dangerously enticing underwater sinkhole – was a quick jeep or camel ride away.

Elka yawned and rubbed her hand over her face. The journey to Dahab had taken nearly 24 hours. She'd managed to get some sleep on her first-class flight to Cairo, but her connection to Sharm El_Sheik and private transfer to the Paradise had been spent going over the case in her head and planning her moves.

Much as she'd wanted to take a nap after she checked in she needed to acquire her targets. Instead of asking questions at the desk, she'd casually mentioned her "friends," Mr. and Mrs. de Ville who were honeymooning, to the bellhop who escorted her to room 205. Obligingly he told her they were on the same floor and had been dining regularly at the hotel.

Once in her room she'd hooked on to the Wi-Fi for a video chat with Tami, her assistant, back at the Agency Confidential offices.

"You look crappy," Tami said cheerfully. "Love that fuzzy hairdo."

Elka touched her short blond locks. Traveling was rough on a girl's looks. Not that Elka was vain. The statuesque woman with the brilliant violet eyes knew she turned men's heads wherever she went, but after one horrific relationship she had decided that she would never again form an attachment. Men were merely for casual dating and hot sex, and there were plenty of them available for that.

"And how come you're so perky? It must be after midnight back in the USA."

"I took a nap so I could be available at your time."

"Well, take another. There's nothing to report yet. I'm going to clean up a bit then see if I can find the de Villes. I'll check back later."

That said, Elka had stripped off her grimy clothes and stepped into the shower. The water flowed in a light spray. Elka sighed; it was typical of the plumbing in many countries. Still, she lathered her body, massaging the tight areas around her neck until the muscles began to relax and she felt revived.

Down in the lobby she drifted around as any tourist might, gathering information on dive trips and safaris offered through the hotel. She wandered out to the pool, moving casually, while her eyes darted about, searching for the couple she had come to find.

She admired the small hotel. Two floors embraced a large circular pool, lit up now in the dark evening like an enormous jewel. A group of four people were seated beneath one of the floodlit palms. Deep in conversation, they paid no attention to Elka as she walked past them to the Fardousse restaurant, which was situated beneath a

14

pavilion adjacent to the sea. Soft lighting and artful placement of shrubbery gave it a romantic air, and for one fleeting moment it struck Elka that it would be a lovely place to share with someone special.

The maître d' bustled up, guiding her to a table on the water's edge.

"Just a glass of white wine, please." Elka positioned herself so she could see the hotel entrance, and all who entered or exited. She wouldn't order dinner until she had eyes on the de Villes.

Ah, there they were; strolling arm in arm across the sand. At first glance you might think them a loving couple. Pay closer attention and you'd notice a controlled arrogance in the young man's manner and a possessive bearing towards his wife. His arm around her waist was just a little too tight; when she began to speak to him he cut her off, his voice clearly heard across the beach saying, "What is wrong with you?"

Without waiting for assistance, they seated themselves at a table close to Elka. The staff bustled up to take care of them and he ordered for them both, in an arrogant, demanding tone.

"A bully," thought Elka. She would have liked to be a little less conspicuous – there were only a handful of guests in the restaurant – but was grateful to be within hearing distance of the couple's conversation. They spoke little, though, and when they did it was desultory. So it was with relief that they left as soon as they'd eaten and returned to their room. Elka followed discreetly, heard the lock engage and retreated to her own room, taking time only to discard her clothes and set the alarm before falling into the bed.

Four

Jase de Ville was adjusting his wife's dive gear. His movements were impatient while Megyn stood, hugging herself, and bore his ministrations. Apparently satisfied, he grabbed her arm and drew her along the beach toward a faded, hand-painted sign on a rickety wooden frame that announced:

EASY ENTRY
BLUE HOLE

From the sign it was just a few feet to the sink hole itself. Megyn hesitated, her uncertainty, her fear in fact, almost palpable to Elka who watched from the cover of one of the open-sided wooden shops – this one selling hand-woven rugs – that lined the beach. Megyn, however, was no match for Jase's will and in short time they disappeared below the water's surface.

Elka hurried after them. Earlier that morning, after she'd downed a small pot of strong, black coffee and breakfasted on local fruit and ta'amiya - the Egyptian version of falafel - she'd hit the dive shop. There she rented a neoprene wetsuit, tanks with trimix breathing gas and all the other gear she might need for a safe dive.

Entering the water, Elka slipped on her mask and allowed herself to sink. Light from above reflected colors of red, orange and yellow off the coral formations lining the hole. At about 150 feet there was nothing but blue and she

17

stopped her descent, looking around for the de Villes. She knew in about 30 more feet she would come to The Arch, a tunnel that led out to the open sea. There, a diver was in darkness and strong currents could grab at you. Even the most experienced divers could find themselves in trouble. In fact, more than 130 people were said to have died in the Blue Hole in the last 15 years.

Movement caught her eye in the shadows below. The de Villes? But no, it was two other divers making their ascent. With signals they asked if she needed help. She signaled OK, then brought out her underwater writing slate and scribbled, "Have u seen a couple?" The two guys responded they'd just seen someone entering The Arch. Elka sped away, praying she wasn't too late.

At the tunnel entrance she switched on the dive light that was strapped to her wrist. Fish wriggled past her. The silence was omnipresent. Then at the edge of the light something came into view. Elka powered forward.

Megyn was thrashing on the tunnel floor. There was no sign of her husband.

Elka couldn't know for sure, but thought it most likely Megyn was suffering nitrogen narcosis. Any diver can be affected, but for someone inexperienced like Megyn the confusion it brought on could easily turn to panic. And people in a state of panic do irrational things, so Elka quickly scratched a note on her slate and approached warily. She reached out and gave the woman several urgent taps on the shoulder. It was enough to startle Megyn into turning her face toward her rescuer. In the next instant she snatched at Elka's arm, but Elka had anticipated the move and was out of reach, holding up her message.

BE STILL
I'LL HELP

Again, Megyn lunged for Elka but she held the slate before her, finger pointing at the words, hoping to focus Megyn's attention. It wasn't working so she lit up her face with the lantern and gave an OK sign. At last, Megyn went still.

Elka glanced at her dive watch. She'd been underwater for 25 minutes. She had plenty of time left with her trimix gas and double tanks, but Megyn had only a single tank and Elka didn't want to assume it contained trimix. She checked the other woman's pressure gauge; it was getting low. They needed to move.

Elka took firm hold of Megyn under the arm, tugging her back to the tunnel entrance, but the woman struggled to move. Panic can be exhausting but something else struck Elka and she unsnapped Megyn's weight belt. Sure enough, there was way too much lead in it. As soon as it was released, Megyn propelled them both forward.

Keeping a firm hold on her charge, Elka brought them to 100 feet and checked the air cylinder again. Should be enough time left to add in a couple of decompression stops, and already Megyn had recovered some of her composure. Nitrogen narcosis typically reverses as the diver returns to a shallower depth, with no long-term effects.

Just as the women breached the surface, several of the locals jumped in to help. They'd been alerted to a possible problem by the two guys Elka had seen earlier.

Eager hands reached out to her but she waved them off, as a voice cried out, "Megyn!"

Jase de Ville ran to his wife, enfolding her in his embrace and immediately taking over the situation, calling for medical assistance and ordering the onlookers to back away.

While all eyes were on the commotion, Elka quietly slipped away.

The following morning Elka again rose early. Megyn de Ville had been taken to the hyperbaric medical center in Dahab. Knowing she would be monitored for hours, possibly overnight, there was little for Elka to do other than return to the Paradise, where she watched for the de Ville's return. When there was no sign of them as the evening drew on, she headed for her room.

At breakfast she got into conversation with the attentive waiter, commenting she'd heard there had been an accident at the Blue Hole.

"Yes, madam," the waiter shook his head sadly. "One of our guests here. The lady was very lucky; many people have died there. Often the bodies are not recovered."

"Do you know what happened?"

He looked around to be sure no-one was near and lowered his voice to a conspiratorial whisper, "We are not encouraged to speak of such things, you understand. But my cousin is one of the guides at the Blue Hole and he tells me the air in the lady's tank was not the proper mix. The young husband, he is very angry and accused Youssef, who provided the tanks, of making a mistake. Youssef insists someone must have changed the tanks without him knowing."

"Is that possible?"

"Youssef has a wife and three children to provide for. Why would he be so careless and risk his business? No, I am telling you he did nothing wrong."

Elka thanked her unwitting informant and applied herself to her meal. A couple of hours and several cups of coffee later there was still no sign of the de Villes, so she wandered to the reception.

"Good morning, Miss Dahl," the young man at the desk gave a cheerful greeting.

"I've been wondering how Mrs. de Ville is. We've become quite friendly," she lied, "and I'm worried I've not heard from her after her accident."

"Oh, she and Mr. de Ville have left the hotel. There was a request last night that their belongings be sent to the airport. I'm afraid I don't know anything else. Perhaps she will contact you later."

Elka turned her head so the receptionist wouldn't see the flash of anger that crossed her face. A moment later she smiled at him. "That's such a shame. I wanted to tell her goodbye because I have to leave myself."

"I'm sorry to hear that, Miss Dahl. I hope your stay with us has been a pleasant one?"

"It has, but would you prepare my bill and call for the car to take me to Sharm El Sheik?"

Five

The rain was beating down as Elka paid off the taxi and stepped to the door of Agency Confidential. It was only seven-thirty in the evening but the weather had driven people off the streets and it was dark and dismal.

Keying in the entry code Elka pushed open the door and was startled by a sudden blur of movement at her feet. She looked down to see a very wet little cat – kitten, really – who in turn looked up at her and gave one long and loud meow.

"Where on earth did you come from?"

She peered up and down the street. There was no-one there. Unsure what she should do, the kitten on the other hand had no doubts. He was already at the top of the stairs waiting for the next door to be opened.

The Agency Confidential offices occupied the space above three shops; all of which Elka owned. The top floor was her apartment. With resignation, and concern for the little animal, Elka trudged upward.

The return journey from Egypt had been even longer than the outgoing. Frustration at losing the de Villes made it impossible for Elka to relax and now she was simply exhausted. Coping with a bedraggled kitten would keep her from her bed a little longer, but there was no way she would ever ignore a creature in need.

Entering the apartment Elka's hand automatically reached out to touch a bronze figurine on a pedestal against the wall. It was the Norse goddess of love, Freyja, and

Elka's personal talisman from which she drew the strength of her Viking ancestors. The kitten sat himself down and immediately began grooming.

"Make yourself at home, why don't you?" Elka was amused at the kitten's brazen inclination to treat the home as if it were his own.

"I suppose you might be hungry. There's sure to be a can of tuna somewhere." She opened a cupboard in the kitchen. "Ah, yes. And it's even organic." By the time she forked half the can into a small dish and set it on the floor the little cat was waiting and tucked right in.

Elka took a moment to scan through her messages but there was nothing that couldn't wait 'til morning. Something else did occur to her, however, and she popped back down to the office, returning with a cardboard box and shredded paper. Grabbing a large trash bag she spent two minutes combining everything then picked up the kitten, who had been busily washing his paws. She plopped him in the paper-filled box.

"This is your litter box," she told him firmly. He looked up at her with dazzling blue eyes then began scratching around and promptly lay down in the nest he'd created and went to sleep. With a sigh Elka decided she'd done all she could for the night and prepared herself for her own bed.

Six

"So what are we going to call him?" Tami was throwing bits of scrunched up paper for the kitten to chase.

"I'm sure he already has a name and we'll find out what it is when we find his owner. You'll be taking him to the vet this morning to check for a microchip and make sure he's in good health. Before that," Elka gave her assistant a hard look, "let's talk about the de Ville's."

"I checked the financials." Tami was a genius on the internet and could hack into just about any account. "Her mother's money passed to Megyn through a living trust, handled by her attorney, so there was no lengthy probate. It doesn't appear that Megyn has a will, but the money would automatically revert to her husband as her only surviving relative."

"How much are we talking about?"

"As best I can say, in the region of thirty million."

"That's a hell of a motive for murder."

"You really think the husband tried to kill Megyn?"

"I know it. I saw him practically force her to make the dive, and he had to know she was much too inexperienced for it. And where was he when she was in trouble? He must have led her in to the tunnel and then abandoned her there. I found out later he claimed she was the one who took off, but she would never have gone off on her own."

"But the tank?"

"It wouldn't have been difficult to exchange the tank for one with compressed air. Everyone is focused on the water, and anyway it's perfectly normal for a diver to pick up a scuba tank. I fear for Megyn. We have to find her and get her away from him."

"Well, I can help you with that. As you requested I sent Agent Brenna to watch the de Ville house. Late yesterday she reported the couple have returned. To maintain cover she is some distance from the house but she took pictures." Tami swiveled her monitor round and Elka bent forward to look at the images.

"That's them." She straightened up again, chewing on her lip in thought. "Send Agent Siri to join Brenna. I want twenty-four hour surveillance on the pair. And get Isabell Kalb on the phone right away."

"On it boss."

Minutes later Elka had brought Isabell up to date. "Can you help me find a way to meet with Megyn? Short of abducting her the only way to keep her safe is convince her that her husband is planning to kill her."

"Hmm. We haven't spoken since before they married. Jase has kept her away from everybody. I suppose I can call and say I'll be in the area and suggest we get together."

"Do it. There's nothing to lose."

Elka hit the off button on the speaker. With elbows on the desk she cradled her head in her hands and drew in a few deep breaths. She hit the speaker again. "Tami, I'm going upstairs for a while."

"OK, boss. I'm heading out soon with the kitten so I'll have calls sent to the service."

"Fine."

She pushed herself to her feet and took the stairs. The apartment was basically one huge loft with a single bedroom and a large workout room containing a punching bag and a variety of weight machines. Elka ignored them, though, and pulled out a yoga mat. She stripped down to her underwear. Picking up a remote she dialed in some numbers. The heat kicked in and the sound system came to life. Rather than traditional yoga music it was a mix of her own favorites, from Procol Harum's "A Whiter Shade of Pale" to Coldplay's "Paradise."

She settled herself in easy pose and began to concentrate on her breathing and allow the music to take her to a restful state.

Seven

Elka entered the bistro. It had an old village French feel with stone walls and blue checked tablecloths.

"Just one for lunch?" The greeter addressed her.

"I'm meeting friends," she said, looking round the small interior and spotting Isabell facing her way, with another woman seated opposite her. She wove across the floor 'til she stood by the women. "Hello, Megyn," she said, "I'm Elka."

Recognition flooded Megyn's features. "You're the one from the Blue Hole."

She jumped up and threw her arms around Elka, who accepted the embrace awkwardly before gently pushing Megyn back into her chair and seating herself between the two women.

"I can't believe you're here," Megyn said. "I never imagined I'd see you again and I have so much to thank you for."

"You can thank me by listening to what I have to say."

"Of course." Megyn's excitement was palpable. "But who are you? How is it that you happen to be here?"

Elka and Isabell exchanged glances.

"What?" Megyn asked. "Do you know each other? Is that why you wanted to meet?" She turned to Isabell and two small creases appeared between her brows. Her voice took on a sudden note of suspicion. "You said you had some mementos of Mom's to give me."

Isabell stretched an arm across the table and gripped Megyn's hand. "I'm sorry, Megyn. The truth is you're in great danger, and Elka and I want to help you."

Megyn snatched her hand away and clasped it to the other in her lap. Shoulders hunched forward and chin down she looked more like a petulant teenager than a cultured young woman. "That's crap. No-one wants to hurt me."

"Your husband does," Elka said.

Megyn's head whipped around, eyes huge in a pinched white face.

"He switched your scuba tank for one with compressed air instead of trimix," Elka continued. "Then he made you dive, didn't he? Even though you were afraid."

"I wasn't afraid."

"I saw your fear, Megyn. Here's what I think happened. Jase made you keep descending. Then because you didn't have the right mix of gases in your tank you started to get light-headed and confused. He took advantage of that to lead you into the Arch, the tunnel, and then he left you."

"That's not true. He would never leave me. You're making this up!" Megyn was becoming more and more agitated.

"It is true," Elka persisted, "and you know it's true. Tell me this: do you remember when I found you it was hard for you to move? You tried to swim with me but you felt really heavy?"

Megyn just glared.

"Extra pockets of weight had been added to your belt. Only Jase could have done that. There were at least fifty pounds of weight that shouldn't have been there."

Shock painted Megyn's face. "No!" She pushed away from the table knocking over her chair. Her voice was shrill. "It's a lie. It's all a lie. Maybe *you* tried to kill me."

"Don't be ridiculous, Megyn." Isabell tried to be reasonable. "What reason could Elka possibly have for doing you harm?"

But Megyn was beyond reason. "Jase loves me. He loves me. He would never hurt me." And with that she rushed from the restaurant as customers looked on askance.

Elka ran after her, catching hold of her arm as she reached the street. "Wait, Megyn. Please."

Megyn struggled to pull away from her grip.

"Take my card," Elka said and shoved it into a pocket of the young woman's jeans. "If you ever need help – ever – call me." With that she let go and Megyn scurried away, shouting over her shoulder, "He loves me."

"Well that certainly didn't go as hoped." Isabell had followed Elka from the bistro and the two women watched as Megyn rounded a corner and disappeared from view.

"I'm afraid we may have made things worse. She's determined not to believe anything bad about her husband." Elka looked grim. Sighing, she gave a tight-lipped smile. "We're not giving up, though." She held out her hand to Isabell. "I'll be in touch if we turn up anything new."

The women shook. "Thanks," Isabell said, and they went their separate ways.

Eight

"Boss, I need you right now." Tami's voice came through the intercom. Elka hurried to the reception area.

"See who's here."

A phalanx of monitors lined the back of the reception desk. Visible to staff but not visitors they showed live feed of every entry into the Agency Confidential building, most of which were unknown except to a chosen few. The main door itself was quite discreet and standing there right now was Jase de Ville, staring straight into the camera.

"He asked to see you. I told him you only saw people by appointment but he said he thought you would make an exception for him. He's horribly smug."

"Perhaps that cocky attitude will make him careless. Let's see what he has to say. Allow him in and put him in the small conference room. He can't do any damage there and he can stew for a half hour or so."

"You got it."

De Ville got to his feet and stepped in front of Elka as she entered the room, effectively blocking her from going forward. A frisson of anxiety shook her but she refused to let it take hold. Instead, she took a half step closer, simultaneously pushing the door closed behind her and drawing herself up to her full height. With her heels she had a three or four inch edge over the man. "Why don't you take a seat, Mr. de Ville," she said, lacing her voice with scorn.

De Ville's features tightened in anger. *He's not used to being bested. Good!* Abruptly he turned away. Settling himself into a chair he crossed his legs and flung an arm over the back in a casual pose and waited for Elka to sit across from him.

"What can I do for you, Mr. de Ville?"

He flung Elka's business card at her on the table: the card she'd given Megyn. "You can leave my wife alone."

"Is she not able to speak for herself?"

"She has me to do that for her."

"And did you speak for your first wife, Megyn's mother? Or did she stand up to you and so you had to kill her?"

He drew his mouth into a thin line. "You'll have to do better than that. Do you think I don't know you must be recording this?" He stood, placing both hands on the table and leaning over so, this time, he was looking down at Elka. "I recognize you now. Megyn told me you were the one at the Blue Hole, but you were staying at the Paradise, weren't you? Were you following us?"

In a strident voice he continued, "Miss Dahl, my wife does not wish to speak with you again. If you try and contact her you'll be having a conversation with my attorney, not me. And for the record, I did not kill my first wife, and Megyn and I are very much in love."

Then he leaned even closer, so Elka could feel the warmth of his breath on her cheek and whispered, "And you'll never prove otherwise."

Sitting in an easy chair, legs curled under her, Elka was sipping a glass of chilled Piper Heidsieck. She liked to say that champagne made everything better and Tami had hurried to bring some to her when she saw that the meeting with de Ville had shaken her boss.

"I felt I was looking into the face of a cobra, waiting for it to spit venom," Elka said. "And like a cobra there is something hypnotic about the man. I haven't felt that since... well, you know."

Tami was the *only* one who knew about the man who had abused Elka as a teenager. It was a subject that was never spoken of, and the reason Elka had started Agency Confidential as a resource for women in need.

"You've still turned up nothing new on de Ville?"

Tami blew out a deep sigh. "It's as if he didn't exist more than a few years ago. I'll keep trying."

"I need you to try harder. Find me something; anything. Meanwhile, arrange for me to talk to the people who saw Pamela Albritton swimming the morning she drowned."

"On it, boss."

Elka went up to her loft. She felt unsettled; usually a heavy workout was enough to release her tension. Today she had a need for something more intimate and was debating between calling Jared, an anesthesiologist or Valentin, a wrestling coach.

Physical stamina and manual dexterity were necessary qualities in an anesthesiologist, and were equally advantageous in a lover. As a wrestler Valentin had tremendous strength and some interesting moves, but he was beginning to get attached. For Elka that was a signal to get out. Men were for physical enjoyment. Friendship was fine, but she wanted no deep emotional involvement. So that settled it; she'd call Jared.

First she'd better check on the kitten. For the time being he was shut in the bedroom - the loft was huge, with too many hiding places – where he'd be safe.

Tami had returned from the vet with news that the kitten was a Snowshoe. A quite rare breed, similar in looks to a Siamese but with four white paws. According to the veterinarian he was five to six months old and had nerve damage in his lower spine that prevented him from jumping. He had not been microchipped.

"The vet thinks a breeder might have dumped him because, with the injury, he has no commercial value," Tami had relayed to Elka. "He's otherwise fine and in no pain."

The kitten was in the middle of the bed. *How on earth…?* Then she noticed the pulled threads on her two thousand dollar Frette quilt.

"You clawed your way up didn't you?" Elka curled up next to the sleeping cat and with one finger tapped him gently on the head. "Are you listening to me? 'Cause you're in big trouble." The kitten responded by wrapping his paws around her finger and purring madly. Elka laughed softly and pulled him to her heart. "It's lucky you're so damn cute. Know what? I don't need Jared. You and I are going to spend the evening together, which means, I guess, that you're here to stay."

As it was, Elka's plans were disrupted anyway when an urgent call came in from Agent Brenna.

"The police and paramedics have just arrived at the de Ville house. Megyn has been there all day. The husband got back about half an hour ago." Brenna paused. "It looks bad."

Nine

"I appreciate you seeing me at such short notice." Elka addressed Esmie and Frank Harding as they sat on the patio of their lake home, looking across the water to the de Ville home. Esmie looked like someone who laughed a lot, with wrinkles in all the right places, but at this moment her features were tight and a hard glint was in her eyes.

"We'd known Pam Albritton since she was born," Esmie said. "We moved here right after we married. There were only a handful of houses on the lake then, and we were all friends. Frank and I were never lucky enough to have children, so we took a special interest in Pam. She was such a sweet child."

Esmie gazed off into the distance, lost in her memories for a few moments. Elka was about to prompt her when she sighed and went on. "We were at the welcome party, you know? Where Pam introduced Jase then told us all to leave. It was dreadful. I said to Frank then that we'd lost her."

"What do you mean?" Elka asked.

"It was obvious she was besotted by him. And Jase, well, he was so condescending, downright rude actually, but Pam dismissed us, all her old friends, as if he was the only thing that mattered."

"Can you tell me about the day she died? You saw her swimming didn't you?"

This time it was Frank who spoke. "We like to go out in the boat fishing. There's a lot of catfish and carp in the lake but sometimes we'll hook a yellow perch. We always throw them back. Time was we'd keep a couple to cook up..."

Esmie leaned over and gently tapped Frank's wrist. He gave her a confused look. "Pam," she said. "Remember we were talking about Pam."

His expression cleared. "Oh, yes... Pam. We often saw her swimming and she would hang on to the side of the boat and chat for a few minutes. She'd been avoiding us, though, since the party, so we were surprised..."

"And happy," Esmie injected.

Frank bobbed his head in agreement, "...when she stopped that morning."

"What did she say?"

Esmie took over from her husband. "Just normal stuff. She asked if we'd had any luck, we asked how the water was; that sort of thing."

"There was nothing that seemed out of the ordinary?" Elka probed. "She didn't seem upset or anxious?"

"Not at all. In fact, we took it as a good sign that she was ready to talk again. And we saw Jase on the deck while she was with us."

"You're sure it was him?"

"Well, I'd think Pam would know her own husband, don't you? He waved and we all waved back. We asked about Megyn, and Pam said she'd gone shopping. That was it. Soon after, we came in."

Elka questioned the Hardings for a while more, but they had nothing else to add so she bade her goodbyes.

"Are you sure you can't stay for a cup of tea or some lemonade?" Esmie looked disappointed. "We don't get many visitors these days."

"I must get back. I'm sorry." Elka thanked the couple and left, feeling as if she was abandoning old friends.

Ten

Agents Siri and Brenna were waiting for Elka at a table in the same bistro where she'd previously met Isabell Kalb with Megyn. Both women stood as their chief approached but she waved them down and sat with them.

"What do you have for me?" Elka's tone was abrupt, which told the women she was tense.

Brenna took the lead. "Megyn's body was taken from the house at eleven thirty-two, several hours after crime scene investigators arrived. The authorities were all gone by midnight. We never saw Jase.

"This morning I was told that Megyn drowned in the bath tub. Supposedly she downed a bunch of sleeping pills with a bottle of champagne, and whether by accident or design slipped under the water. Jase found her when he got home."

"Just who was it who told you this?"

"A journalist who has an informer in the police department." In response to Elka's raised eyebrows, Brenna added, "I'm sure he's telling me what he believes to be true. He thinks I really find nerdy crime reporters hot."

There was silence. Then Elka burst out laughing. In addition to being smart and capable, her agents were all incredibly sexy women; and they knew how to use that to their advantage.

Elka drew in a deep breath and put her serious face back on. "This is no accident, nor is it a suicide. That bastard murdered Megyn as surely as he murdered her mother, and we need to prove it before he kills again.

"Brenna, stay here and see if your journalist can come up with any more information. Siri, you'll return to the office with me."

The three women rose together and left the restaurant. Elka couldn't help but remember standing in the same place pleading with Megyn to get away from Jase. Once again a sense of guilt crept into her psyche. Had she pushed him to kill quickly?

I'll get you, you bastard. One way or another, I'll get you.

Eleven

"I found him!" Tami was exultant. "It finally occurred to me to try variations of Jase de Ville and there he was. His real name is Jason Deville but he changed it after a girlfriend of his died."

"Whoa!" Elka threw her hands up. "Let me at least get in the door; then start at the beginning."

She'd just got back to the office after dropping Siri off and her mind was still racing with thoughts of Megyn's death. She crossed to the refrigerator and grabbed a bottle of cold water, downing it in one. Then rubbed the knots in her neck and shoulders and took a few deep breaths. "OK, now tell me what you found."

Calmer now, Tami gave her boss succinct details. "Jason Deville was eighteen years old when his girlfriend 'supposedly' dove off a dock and hit her head on the bottom, was knocked unconscious and drowned. There were no eye witnesses other than Deville, or *de* Ville, who claimed he went in after her when she didn't surface, but by the time he found her it was too late.

"And get this. The girlfriend was pregnant."

Elka's lips formed a tight line. "He probably killed the girl so he wouldn't have to deal with a baby."

"It's looking that way, but I have more."

"Go on," Elka said.

"Once I knew the name I just kept working backward and I found a short article about a four-year-old boy who'd drowned. He'd been underwater for more than

45

an hour when he was found, his body tangled in pondweed. The water temperature was less than forty degrees and before pronouncing him dead efforts were made to bring his temperature back up and revive him. Amazingly, he survived."

"And this was de Ville?"

"Right. And remember Isabell said he had a sea serpent tattoo? Well, the article quoted the boy's parents as saying he told them that snakes were holding him."

"Shit. I guess to a little kid who's dying, pond weed could easily seem like snakes – or serpents. No wonder he has an obsession with drowning." She paused, lost in thought for a few moments. "And how many more women might have died because of it?"

Twelve

It was a somber group who gathered at the de Ville house this time, though the champagne was being poured liberally. Elka stood off to the side with Isabell, watching Jase de Ville work the room like a preening peacock. She'd been surprised when he'd issued an open invitation to one and all to attend what he called "A celebration of the life of his beloved wife."

According to Isabell, most of the attendees had been at the original party, including the Hardings. They greeted Elka warmly, and in the background Jase gave her a sly smile, letting her know he was aware she'd talked to them before.

"There's Bud," Esmie Harding lifted a hand in greeting to a slender, fiftyish man whose stooped frame looked as if it was breaking under the weight of the world. As he reached them Esmie said, "Elka, this is our Chief of Police, Bud Babiak. Bud, meet..."

"I know who Ms. Dahl is." He caught her by the elbow and steered her away from the others. "Thank you for the information you sent."

"Has it been of help?"

Babiak snorted through his nostrils. "It's confirmed my suspicions there's more to these deaths and to Mr. de Ville than meets the eye, but I need actual proof of a crime."

Elka had sent her complete case file to Babiak in hopes he might have something to add to it that would implicate de Ville. Apparently that was not to be.

"According to the husband his wife was depressed over her mother's death and had been having difficulty sleeping. Hence the pills."

"There was no forensic evidence to suggest foul play?"

"Not so far. We're still working the case; I know this bastard is dirty but he's also clever. He pulled the wife out of the tub to try and revive her – so he says. In doing so, he broke the champagne bottle and got soapy water everywhere. My gut tells me he killed her, but that won't put him behind bars."

A clinking of glass got their attention. A man stood in the center of the room, arm raised, calling out, "Everyone, please, I'd like to say a few words." He was wearing a Panama bowler hat, drawn down over one eye. As Elka wondered who it was he raised the hat high and waved it to his audience. "A hat can easily change a person's appearance, can't it?" Jase tossed the bowler aside, looking directly at Elka, and grinned. She drew in a sharp breath and the color drained from her face as the enormity of what he'd just said hit her.

She hurried back to Isabell and the Hardings as the noise died down to a rustle and Jase began a eulogy.

"Esmie," she whispered, "when you were in the boat talking to Pam, and de Ville waved from the deck, was he wearing a hat?"

"Yes. The same one he just had on. He wears it often." She frowned. "Are you alright, dear? You look rather pale."

"Excuse me." Elka strode stiffly from the room, flung wide the front door, slamming it shut behind her then smacking her hand against the frame. "Damn, damn, damn, damn, damn!"

The door opened and Isabell stepped through. "What the hell happened to you?"

"De Ville just told us how he did it," Elka spat.

Isabell grabbed her by the shoulders. "Calm down! " I didn't hear him saying anything about killing Megyn."

"Not Megyn. Pam!" Elka shrugged away from Isabell's grip and took in a deep gulp of air, letting it out with a whoosh.

"Don't you see? It's the hat. He made sure to wear it often so everybody associated it with him. When the Hardings and Pam saw someone on the deck they all assumed it was Jase, because of the hat."

"So you're saying it wasn't Jase? But who else could it be?"

"Megyn, of course."

Isabell's face went slack and her eyes wide. "You... you can't be saying Megyn helped Jase kill her mother?"

"That's exactly what I'm saying. It was Megyn on the deck, wearing Jase's hat and clothes, and everyone just assumed it was him."

"Then where was Jase?"

"Underwater. He's a diver; it would have been easy for him to follow Pam and drag her down in the middle of the lake. The timing had to be right because they needed witnesses, and Pam played right into their hands by stopping to talk to the Hardings."

"But surely they would have seen bubbles from de Ville's scuba tank. I know the Hardings are old and might not have noted any significance, but Pam certainly would."

"There wouldn't have been any bubbles." Elka was emphatic. "He would know to use a rebreather."

Isabell's expression was blank.

"It's a closed circuit breathing system that produces no bubbles," Elka explained. "They're popular with underwater photographers because they're also quiet and don't disturb lake or marine life. So there'd be nothing to alarm the Hardings or Pam."

"I knew it." Isabell's face cleared. "I just knew he'd murdered Pam, but how did he convince Megyn to go along with it?"

"Maybe he didn't. He might have told her it was some sort of joke. Either way, we'll probably never know. And there's not a shred of hard evidence he did anything."

"If the rebreather is found, won't that implicate him?"

"Any diver might have one, and with Megyn out of the way there are no witnesses."

"What are you going to do?"

Elka shook her head. "Tell detective Babiak and hope he can use the information to shake de Ville up." She looked at Isabell and was silent for a while. "I'm sorry."

"Don't be ridiculous," Isabell said. "You've done everything you can. Eventually, he'll make a mistake and then he'll be caught."

"How many more women will die before then?" Elka's tone was bitter as she and Isabell stepped back into the house.

Thirteen

"Well?" Tami poked her head into Elka's office. "What did Babiak have to say?" Her boss beckoned her inside. "That was a pretty brief call," she added.

"That's because there was little to tell."

Three months had passed since Megyn had been found dead. Elka had refused to take Isabell's money "...because," she said, "she had failed to save Megyn." To which Isabell had pithily replied, "Megyn knowingly put herself in de Ville's hands. I don't think anyone could have saved her."

"Men like him prey on women who are naïve and vulnerable," Elka said. "I was one of those women once." Then before Isabell had a chance to respond, she changed the subject back to the fee. Finally, the women had agreed on a lesser amount but, unknown to Isabell, Elka continued to have de Ville watched.

Shaking herself from her thoughts Elka gave her attention to her assistant. "Babiak said Megyn's death has now officially been ruled a suicide."

"Shit. How can that be?"

"There's no evidence to prove otherwise. Bruises were found on Megyn's arms and chest that could just have easily been caused by de Ville pulling her out of the tub and giving CPR as holding her down. She had a prescription for the Ambien she took. Whether de Ville persuaded her to take it, or forced her to, there's no way to know. And I had firsthand experience that day at lunch how volatile her mood could be."

Before anything else could be said, the phone rang. All the agent's calls came in on separate lines so they could be instantly identified. Tami leaned across Elka's desk, "Hi, Brenna. Do you have something to report?"

"Put it on speaker," Elka said.

"Boss?"

"I'm here, Brenna."

"Boss, a woman just arrived by taxi at de Ville's house. She has a suitcase with her."

"How big is the suitcase?"

"Bigger than an overnight. It would carry everything a sexy young woman would need for a few days – and nights – of intimacy with a young man."

"I take it she is a sexy young woman."

"Sending a picture now boss."

Tami diverted the image to Elka's monitor and they peered at a pretty brunette standing beside the taxi.

"If I'm not mistaken," Elka squinted, "that's a Valextra case. They're Italian handmade and that one would have cost nothing less than four thousand dollars." She looked at Tami. "This girl reeks of money. I think de Ville has found his next victim."

Fourteen

Oddly enough the bright moonlight might have been an advantage for the intruder. Because of it Jase de Ville hadn't turned on the patio lighting. The lights in the built-in Jacuzzi, however, were rotating through the colors of the rainbow, setting the mood for a romantic sexual interlude.

The intruder, head to toe in black and with a blackened face, was motionless in the shadows of the surrounding trees. Jase had claimed the woman right there in the hot tub. The intruder had watched as he stood in front of her, took her hair in his fist and pulled her mouth over his erection. His lips moved in speech but his voice couldn't be heard over the whirlpool jets. Then he caught her hair in both hands and pumped his arms back and forth so her head bobbed with them, faster and faster.

Just when it looked as if he must come, he withdrew himself and flipped the woman so she lay with her stomach over the side of the spa. He dipped his knees and penetrated her from behind while one hand grabbed and squeezed her left tit, and the other he used to brace himself as he drove into her.

She clung to his forearms with both hands. Her right breast slapped against the side of the tub in rhythm with his thrusts and she cried out; whether in agony or ecstasy the intruder couldn't tell.

When he was done, de Ville pulled away and sat with his arms spread over the back of the Jacuzzi. He lifted his face to the stars and let out a triumphant howl. The girl hung, limp; unmoving, 'til de Ville slapped her buttock and she raised her head to look at him. Again his lips moved with silent words and, wearily, she pushed herself to her feet and stumbled from the hot tub and into the house.

From the safety of the shadows the intruder darted up behind de Ville, one arm wrapping over his face, pinning his head in position, while the other drew a knife swiftly and efficiently from below the left ear across to the right, severing the jugulars, carotid arteries and the windpipe.

Blood spurted from de Ville's neck while his body took giant gasping breaths through the severed windpipe. Then the intruder thrust him down so, instead of air, his lungs drew in bloody water. At that same moment the timer for the jets kicked off. In the immediate silence that followed there was a crash of breaking glass. Looking toward the sound the intruder saw the girl, a broken bottle at her feet, wine glasses held loosely between her fingers. Their eyes connected. The girl's mouth fell open, she flung the glasses away, turned and slammed the door shut behind her. The intruder wiped the knife blade on a nearby towel then, panther-like, walked away from the house.

Fifteen

In the Agency Confidential lounge Elka watched the kitten as he sat in front of the aquarium. He was completely intent on the fish swimming back and forth and occasionally, as one would pass right in front of him, a paw would dart out and smack the glass.

Siri laughed. "He's very determined, isn't he?" She and Brenna were with their chief sitting comfortably around a low table, sipping their boss's favorite Piper Heidsieck champagne. Elka leaned forward and pulled the bottle from the thermoelectric chiller and topped off their glasses.

"You've just helped me decide on a name for him."

"Well, don't keep us in suspense," Siri said. "What is it?"

"Destin," Elka replied. "It's an old Norse name that means 'determined.'"

"Of course it would have to be from the Viking age," Brenna said with a hint of sarcasm.

Elka merely smiled. Her operatives didn't need to understand her affinity with her Viking ancestors or the special bond she felt to the goddess, Freyja, who, she believed, had saved her life. In honor of those forebears – and to preserve anonymity – all of her agents were given fictitious names with singular meaning. Brenna meant "sword," and Siri meant "from the house of strength."

Conversation returned to light-hearted chatter about the kitten when Tami burst through the door.

"You'll never believe what just came on the news!"

Three heads whipped in her direction.

"Jase de Ville was killed last night."

There was a simultaneous gasp. "Was it the woman staying with him?" Brenna asked.

"The only other thing I heard is that he was found in the Jacuzzi."

"My god," Brenna said to her boss, "If you hadn't pulled us from surveillance we might have seen what happened, or even prevented it."

"And how ironic," Siri added, "that he died in water, like his victims. At least, I suppose he must have drowned."

"Yeeess," Tami narrowed her eyes at her boss. "It is remarkable that de Ville died in water, and right after you ended surveillance."

Elka's lips curled in a satisfied smile. "I would call it serendipitous."

The End

If you enjoyed this story, please leave a review. Your words really mean a lot.

And read the first Agency Confidential book:

Deceit

You can be among the first to hear about Liz's new book releases and special deals when you join her email list at the website here: http://www.LizDodwell.com.

Choose Cozy Mystery; Mystery & Adventure, or both.

Liz Dodwell

…was told so many times that she really knew how to spin a story, she finally decided to put that talent to good use.

Liz writes from the home she shares with husband Alex and a crew of rescued dogs and cats. For a change of pace she pens stories in cozy mystery and romantic suspense. For relaxation she likes to yodel. (Just kidding).

You can always reach Liz on her facebook page: facebook.com/LizDodwellAuthor. She'd love to hear from you.

Other books from Liz Dodwell:
- Adventure/Mystery
  - The Mystery of the One-Armed Man
  - Black Bart is Dead
  - The Gold Doubloon Mystery
  - The Game's a Foot
- Cozy Mystery
  - Doggone Christmas
- Romantic Suspense
  - Edge of Never

www.ingramcontent.com/pod-product-compliance
Lightning Source LLC
Chambersburg PA
CBHW071216130626
46555CB00004B/1730